After
High Tide

Story by Dawn McMillan
Illustrations by Roberto Fino

Contents

Chapter 1

No Football for Theo

Cody pulled his football sock over his artificial leg.
When he was four years old,
he had been in a car accident
and one of his legs had been too badly injured to save.
But having an artificial leg didn't stop him
from playing football.
Today, he was playing for his school team.

As Cody ran onto the football field,
he waved to his friend, Theo,
who was sitting at the sideline.

"Make sure you cheer for us, Theo!" Cody yelled.

Theo had wanted to join the school team,
but two weeks ago he had fallen
down the stairs at school and had broken his leg.

After the game, Cody rushed over to sit beside Theo.
"We beat them," he said excitedly.
"I'm glad I got that goal!"

"Me, too!" grinned Theo.

"I wish you'd been able to play today, Theo,"
said Cody.
"You must get so bored sitting around,
waiting for your leg to mend."

Then he smiled secretly, and said,
"But you won't be bored tomorrow!
Dad and I have a surprise for you.
We're coming to get you at eight o'clock.
See you in the morning!"

As Theo watched Cody ride away,
he wondered where they might be going tomorrow.
He really liked Cody.
When Theo was in hospital with his broken leg,
Cody had visited him every day
and they had been friends ever since.

Chapter 2

Are We Going Fishing?

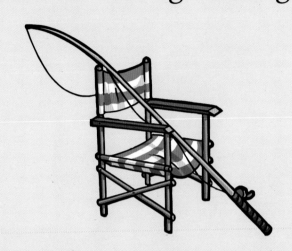

The next morning, Theo was up early.
"I don't want to be late for Cody," he said to his father.

"I don't either," replied Dad.

"Are you coming, too?" asked Theo, looking puzzled.

"Yes," laughed Dad.
"Someone has to eat this apple pie.
I made it last night when you were asleep!"

Suddenly, Theo heard the sound of a car
pulling up in the drive.

"Here they are!" he said, as he looked out the window.
"Dad! They have fishing rods on the top of the car.
Are we going fishing? I love fishing!
But I can't stand with my crutches
and hold a fishing rod."

"Don't worry, Theo," smiled Dad.
"Cody has it all organised for you."

"The tide is coming in," said Cody excitedly,
when they got to the wharf.
"It will be just right for fishing."

Theo was excited, too, and worried.
"I'm not sure how I'm going to do this,"
he said to Cody.

14

"My grandpa has given you his lucky fishing chair
for the day," Cody replied.
"You can sit down and fish, Theo,
but you'd better not catch all the big ones!"

15

Chapter 3

Not Even a Nibble

When everyone had their fishing lines in the water,
Cody stood beside Theo
and they waited for the fish to bite.

Cody's dad and Theo's dad waited, too.

"Not even a nibble," frowned Cody,
as he checked his bait.

About an hour later, Cody's dad called,
"There's no sign of any fish. Let's have some lunch!"

"Yes, please," replied Cody. "I'm hungry!"

After lunch, they all tossed their fishing lines back into the water.

Again, everyone waited and waited.

"There's still no sign of fish!" Cody said with a frown.

Theo smiled and said, "This chair is very comfortable.
I might have a sleep!"

Chapter 4

It's a Big One!

When the tide turned, Cody's dad called,
"Time to go home, boys.
We never catch fish here after the high tide."

But, at that moment, Theo felt something on his line.
The tip of his rod was bending.
"Cody!" he shouted in amazement.
"I think I've got something!"

"Dad!" yelled Cody.
"Come and help! Theo's caught a fish!"

"It must be a big one!" Theo shouted back.

"I can see it! It's almost at the wharf!"
yelled Cody excitedly. "Keep the rod up, Theo!
Get the net, Dad! Quick!"

With a flick of the net,
Cody's dad landed the fish on the wharf.

"It's a good size!" said Theo proudly.

Then he turned to Cody and said with a grin,
"Yesterday you scored a goal and today I caught a fish!"

"Thanks for bringing me fishing, Cody," Theo added.
"Fishing is great, and your grandpa's chair really is lucky!"